TYLER TAMES THE TESTING TIGER

Janet M. Bender, M. Ed.

National Center for Youth Issues, Chattanooga, TN

Tyler Tames the Testing Tiger

ISBN 13: 978-1-931636-27-8

Written by: Janet M. Bender
Cover Design and Layout by Contract: Tonya Daugherty
Contract Illustrator: Tonya Daugherty

Published by:

National Center for Youth Issues
P. O. Box 22185
Chattanooga, Tennessee 37422-2185
1-800-477-8277
www.ncyi.org

Printed in the United States of America

Dedication

This book is dedicated to all the counselors and teachers who coordinate and administer tests, always remembering that a child's worth is never measured by a test score.

About the Author

Janet Bender is a veteran author, presenter and consultant in the field of elementary counseling. A former elementary teacher and school counselor, she has applied her 30 years experience in education to create helpful, practical materials for counselors still working in the field. She resides in Goose Creek, SC with her husband, Frank. You may contact Janet by phone or e -mail: jmbender@wpmedia.net or 843-553-8802.

Other published resources by Janet M. Bender include:

- *Ready... Set... Go! A Practical Resource for Elementary Counselors*

- *School Counselor's Scrapbook*

- *My Daddy is in Jail*

- *Easy as Pie... A Generous Serving of Creative Guidance Presentations (CD-Rom)*

- *Perfect Pals: How to Juggle Your Way From Perfection to Excellence*

Table of Contents

Introduction

Testing is an inevitable part of life. From the classroom to the DMV, we all find ourselves faced with the challenge to perform and be scored against some standard of excellence. Similarly, we all have experienced the anxiety that often accompanies fear of failure on any given measure of our competence.

With growing pressure for accountability, education systems across the country find themselves spending more money, personnel and time administering standardized tests to youngsters from grades K–12. Naturally, teachers, parents and administrators feel the stress and often unintentionally pass it along to students.

Tyler Tames the Testing Tiger addresses the anxiety often felt by students at testing time. It can be used by teachers and school counselors to prepare children for standardized testing by helping students identify their own level of test anxiety and develop strategies for relaxation, positive thinking, time management, study skills, mental and physical preparation, and test taking skills. A helpful parent article is also included.

Using tips learned from his basketball coach, Tyler manages to "tame the testing tiger" by applying successful sports strategies to the testing situation. His success will encourage other students with similar struggles.

Janet M. Bender

The morning bell rang and Tyler walked very slowly down the hallway and into his third-grade classroom. He was usually excited to return to school on Mondays after a weekend apart from his friends. But this Monday was different. Today, everyone in the third grade would begin taking the state achievement test. Tyler had four days of testing ahead of him and he wasn't looking forward to it.

How do you feel about taking tests?

For weeks now, Tyler's teacher, Mrs. Best, had been talking about this test and how important it was to do well on it. Students would be tested in math, reading and writing. Tyler was pretty good in math, but his reading was another story. He liked to listen to stories, but when he tried to read aloud he got nervous and missed lots of words. Tyler remembered from the sample tests Mrs. Best had given that the questions at the end of the story each had four possible answers to choose from. He had a hard time remembering what had happened in the story he had read, so he often got confused when trying to choose an answer. And to make things worse, sometimes he couldn't read or understand all the words in the questions.

When do you get nervous in school?

Which subject is your best?

Is there a subject that is harder for you than the others?

...were us... excited to return... Mondays... and a... in his... at the... M... different. Today,... the third grade would begin taking the state achievement test. Tyler had four days of testing ahead of him and he wasn't looking forward to it.

For weeks now, Tyler's teacher, Mrs. Best, had been talking about this test and how important it was for the school to do well on it. Students would be tested in math, reading and writing. Tyler was pretty good in math, but his reading was another story. He liked to hear stories, but when he tried to read aloud he got nervous and missed lots of words. Tyler remembered from the sample tests Mrs. Best had given that the questions at the end of the story had four possible answers to choose from. He had a hard time remembering what had happened in the story... he often got confused when trying to choose an answer. And to... worse, sometimes he couldn't... words in the question...

And then there was the writing part of the test. On the writing test, Tyler would be given a topic to write about in a limited amount of time. They had practiced this in class many times; but when it came to putting it down on paper at test time, spelling all the words correctly, with the test timer ticking, his mind went blank and he couldn't think of anything to write.

Did you ever have a time when your mind went "blank?"

What else might happen when someone gets very nervous?

Mrs. Best greeted Tyler and the other children and hurried them to their desks with a tense smile— seeming less relaxed than usual. The classroom looked different too. All the desks were spread far apart instead of in the normal groups of four, so it took Tyler a minute or two to find his desk. As he took his seat and looked around the room, he noticed that the walls of the classroom were covered with large sheets of colored paper, which covered up the familiar bulletin boards, charts and displays. This didn't look like the classroom he remembered from last week.

Does your classroom look different on testing days?

How?

Why?

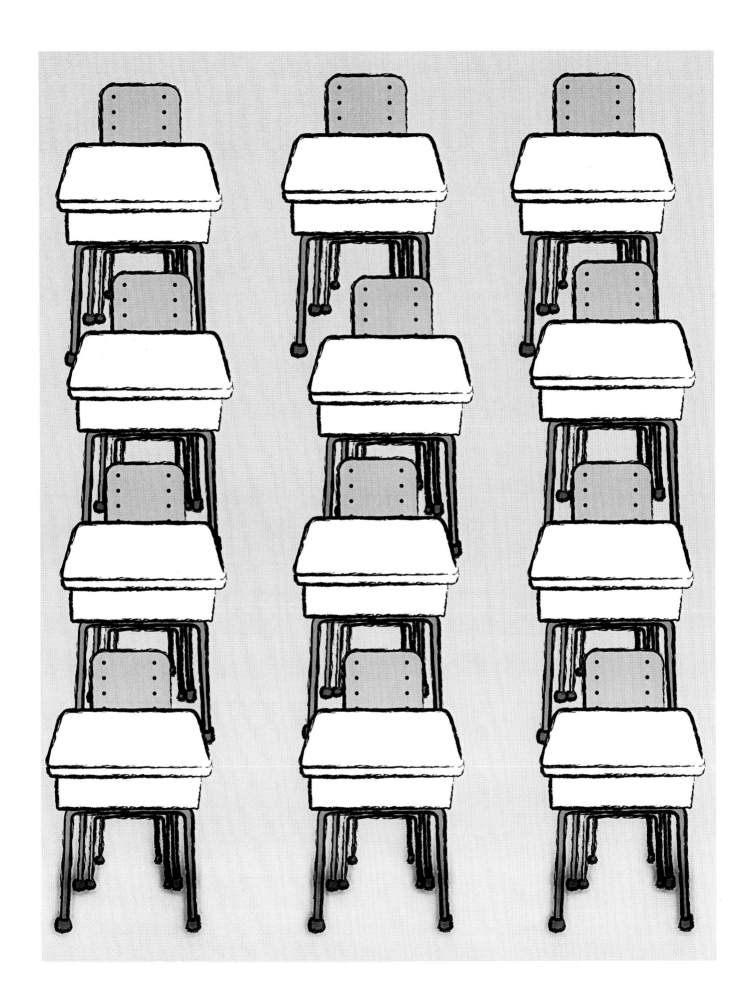

Tyler's stomach tightened as Mrs. Best called the roll and had the students sharpen their two #2 pencils. There was also another grown-up in the class today. Mrs. Best introduced her as a monitor to help during testing. Students were told to raise their hands if they needed another pencil or had any emergency. Otherwise, they were warned not to talk or get out of their seats until the testing was over.

How can you tell that Tyler was nervous about the test?

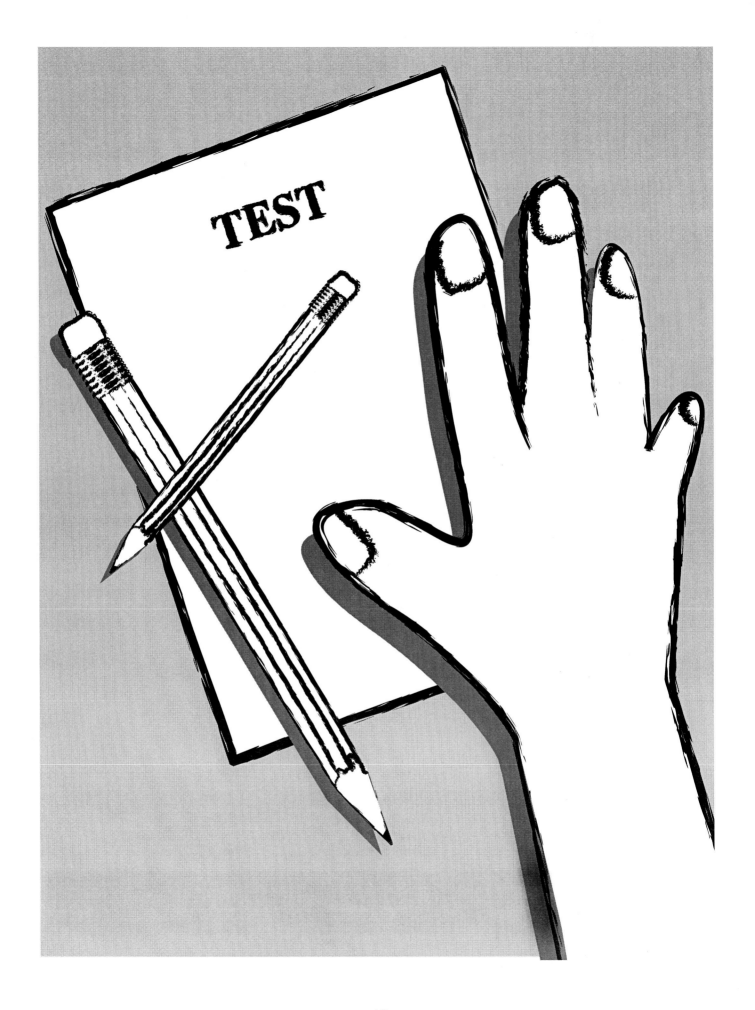

After everyone was settled in their desks with pencils, cover sheets, and test booklets, Mrs. Best began the instructions for Part I of the test. In a slow and serious voice, she told the students to relax and do their best.

Tyler thought, "How can I relax when everything seems so different, and my teacher is acting so weird? This state test must be awful." Tyler imagined the test booklet on his desk as a fearful tiger getting ready to devour him in one bite.

When you're nervous, do you ever imagine unpleasant things?

His stomach flapped like a butterfly, his hands began to sweat, and his heart pounded like a drum. Then, suddenly he remembered something his basketball coach, Mr. Frank, had taught him at practice in the last few weeks.

How does your body react to stress or nervousness?

Tyler usually played well during practice, but at a game with a gym full of screaming spectators he often got nervous and couldn't concentrate on his foul shots. Mr. Frank's tips had helped him relax and perform better in basketball games, so maybe they could help with test-taking, too.

Mr. Frank had shared with Tyler his own technique for dealing with a case of shaky nerves during a basketball game. He suggested that Tyler develop his own way to calm himself before shooting foul shots and repeat the same thing every time he stepped up to the line to attempt a shot.

What helps you relax when you are nervous?

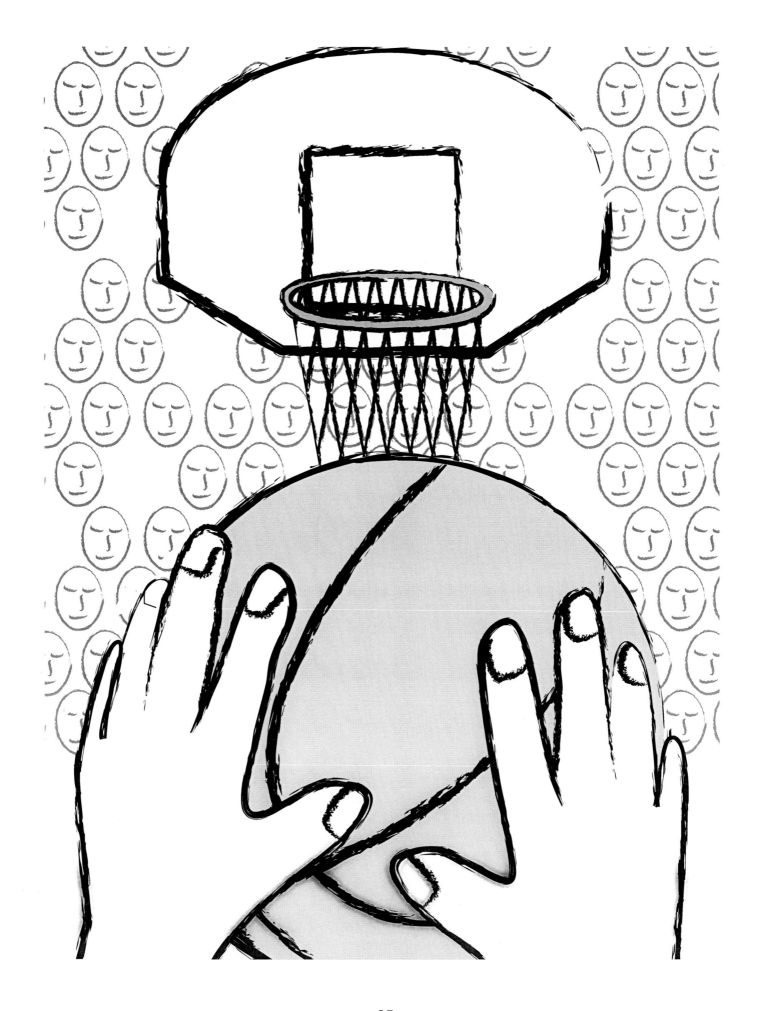

In basketball, the process that seemed to help Tyler was to square off his feet, bounce the ball three times, take a deep breath, let it out, and shoot. If he missed the shot and had another one coming, Tyler had learned to go through his exact steps again. With this routine in place, his foul shooting was improving.

The second thing his coach taught him was to think positively about making each basketball shot. When Tyler approached the basket, he thought to himself, "I'm a good player. I'm gonna make this shot." Before Mr. Frank came along, Tyler thought about how ashamed he would feel if he missed the shot. He had worried that his parents and coaches would think he was a bad player.

Mr. Frank also reassured Tyler that nobody—even the great professional players—makes all of their shots. Everyone makes mistakes. From then on, Tyler tried not to be so hard on himself when he missed a shot or a pass. Getting stuck thinking about the shot he missed, would hurt his concentration on the next shot. He tried to put it out of his head and go on with the game.

Think of a positive message you can say
to yourself when you need to calm down.

Tyler learned the hard way that preparing himself physically for a game also really helped improve his performance. One week, he had a game on Saturday morning at 9:00, and he had spent the night with a friend on Friday. Of course, they had stayed up too late playing video games. On Saturday morning, Tyler had to drag himself out of bed and got to the gym just in time for the game to start. He was too tired to play his very best.

How can you prepare better for tests so you won't be as nervous on test day?

In addition to thinking positively, following his shooting routine, and getting the proper amount of rest, Tyler learned the importance of regular practice. He was discouraged early in the season because he didn't play as well as some of the other boys. Mr. Frank encouraged him to spend extra time after school practicing. Tyler found that practice didn't make him a perfect player, but it sure did improve his performance and his confidence.

Tell about something you can do better after practicing regularly.

In the middle of his basketball daydream, Tyler heard Mrs. Best announce a ten-minute delay in starting the state achievement test due to a late bus. "Great!" he thought. "I'll take this time to get ready for the test." He quickly made a mental list of "coach's tips" to help him relax and do his best on the test.

—1—
Develop a relaxing routine

Tyler put down his pencil, imagined being in his favorite place (his tree house), and slowly took three deep breaths before putting his name on his test booklet.

I develop a relaxing routine

—2—
Talk and Think Positively

Tyler said to himself: "I am a smart
kid and I'm going to do my best."

—3—
Don't Get Stuck

Tyler reminded himself that everybody makes
mistakes. "I don't have to know all the answers.
If I don't know one, I can make my best guess
and go on to the next question" he thought.

1. Develop a Relaxing Routine
2. Talk and Think Positively
3. Don't Get Stuck
I'm a smart kid. I can do this!

—4—
Practice to Make Progress

Tyler reminded himself to read over each question carefully two times before choosing an answer. He also decided to practice reading to his mom and little sister at home to get more comfortable and confident with his reading.

—5—
Prepare Your Body Physically

Tyler promised himself to get to bed early tonight and to eat a healthy breakfast tomorrow morning before coming to school.

Just as Tyler finished his mental list of test-taking tips, he heard Mrs. Best announce that she was ready to begin the test. Much to his surprise, Tyler felt fine now. He had been so busy focusing on his basketball coach's tips that his nervous butterflies had gone away.

How did Tyler's feelings change and why?

He looked down at the test booklet on his desk and saw a harmless green booklet where the fearful tiger had been. Tyler took a deep breath, picked up his pencil, and raised his hand as he smiled at Mrs. Best.

"Yes, Tyler," Mrs. Best replied. "Don't worry, Mrs. Best. You're a great teacher and we're going to do just fine on this test," Tyler said.

"Thanks, Tyler," replied Mrs. Best with a smile. "I needed that."

Tyler smiled and thought to himself, "I guess teachers need to tame tigers sometimes, too."

What is the purpose of standardized tests?

Why do you think students get so nervous about tests?

Why do you think teachers also get nervous about tests?

Do you think you will perform better on tests if you are nervous or calm? Explain your answer.

What have you learned from this story that might help you "tame the testing tiger?"

Leader's Guide

Testing Bulletin Board

Test Prep Cards

Test Anxiety Assessment

Coach's Tips

How Parents Can Help

Testing Bulletin Board

Tame the Testing Tiger

❖ Prepare Your Body

❖ Practice to Make Progress

❖ Relax

❖ Think Positively

❖ Don't Get Stuck

*Adapted from "Tame the Testing Tiger," **School Counselor's Scrapbook,** Youthlight, Inc. 2002.

Test Prep Card #1

Be Prepared!

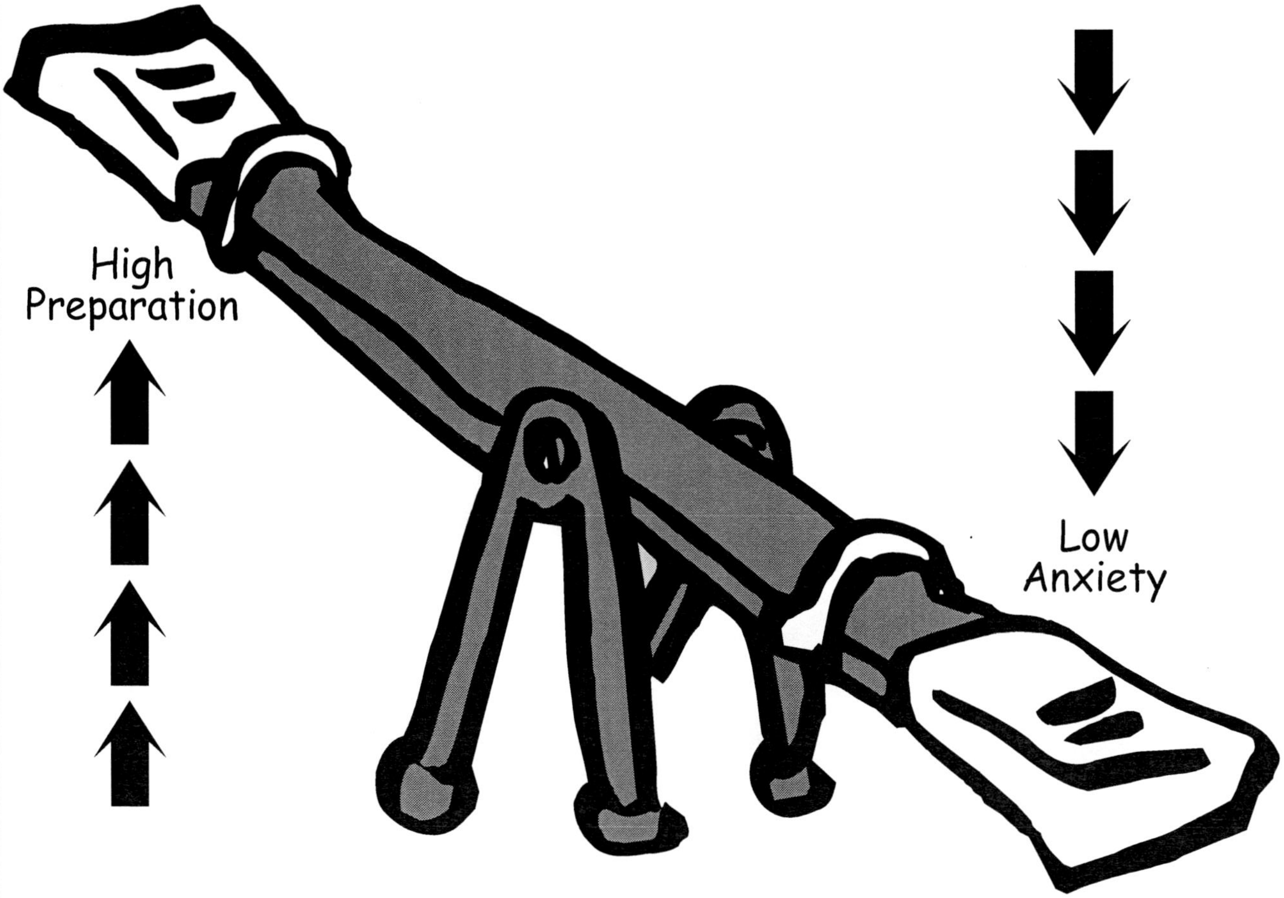

High Preparation = Low Anxiety

Be Prepared!

If you practice a hobby such as piano or baseball,

you're likely to play well on recital or game day.

When you know you have prepared for a

test by studying or practicing the material,

you can relax and do your best.

High Preparation = Low Anxiety

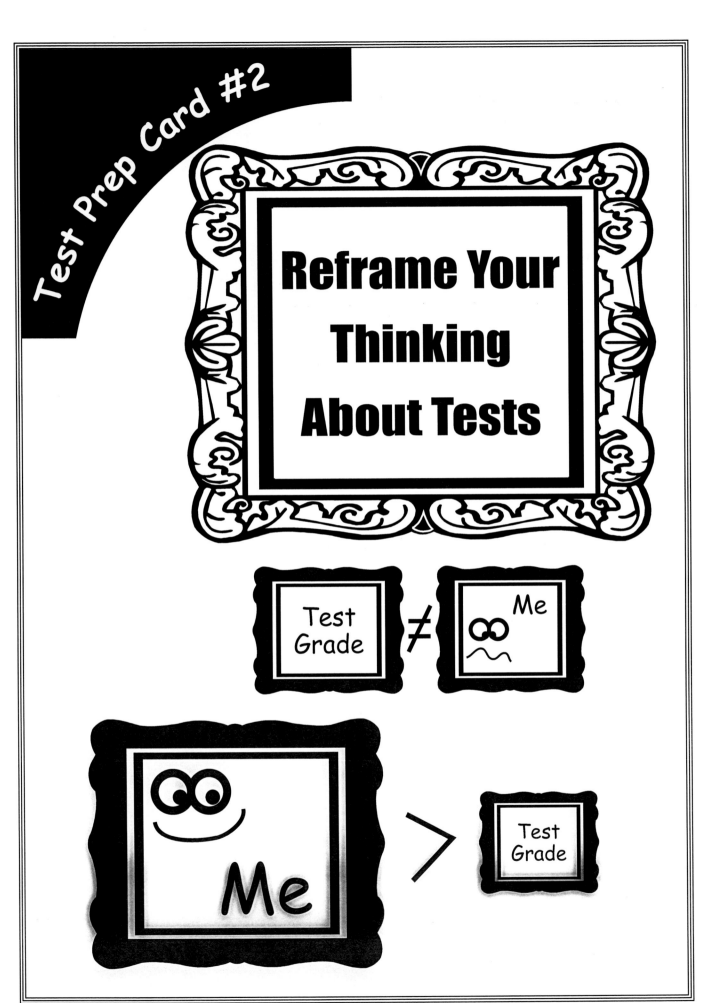

Reframe Your Thinking

Some people think that a poor test grade makes them

a failure or a loser. If you had the flu last month, does

that make you a "sick" person all the time? Of course

not. Try to remember that your performance on

a test is just one small part of who you are.

_____

*Use this simple activity to demonstrate
that a person's behavior is separate
from the person himself.*

*Hold a piece of paper in one hand
and a book in the other. (Or a pencil
and pen, any two objects will do)
Hold up each object as you say:
"This is the behavior (paper).
This is the person (book)."*

*"This is the test grade."
"This is the person."*

Good Listeners...

Stop

their hands & feet are still

Look

their eyes are on the speaker

Listen

think about what they hear

Good Listeners...

STOP what they are doing and keep hands, feet and body still.

LOOK at the speaker.

LISTEN with their ears and think about what is being said.

You listen with your eyes, ears and body.

Fear...
Real or Imagined?

"The only thing you have to fear is fear itself."
—Franklin D. Roosevelt

Fear of Tests

Fear of tests can cause some people to get

nervous and do worse than they normally

would. Think about why you are afraid of tests.

Can a test hurt you like a wild tiger could?

Are you afraid of disappointing others or

embarrassing yourself? Try to relax and remember

that a test can't hurt you, but your own fear can!

(You may want to use the Test Anxiety
Assessment from page 67 with this card.)

Study day-by-day. Don't cram!

55 National Center for Youth Issues, Chattanooga, TN

Studying Ahead

Studies show that most people remember

facts better when they review and repeat

them in several short sessions over time,

rather than trying to cram a lot of information

in one long session the day before the test

Try it, you might be surprised!

Watch the Time

Pace Yourself.
Not too fast... Not too slow.

Pacing Yourself

During a test, try to work at middle speed.

If you work too quickly, you're likely to make

careless mistakes. If you get stuck by working

too long on one hard question, you may get

frustrated or not finish the test. Skip the ones

you aren't sure of, and come back to them later.

Relax With Deep Breathing

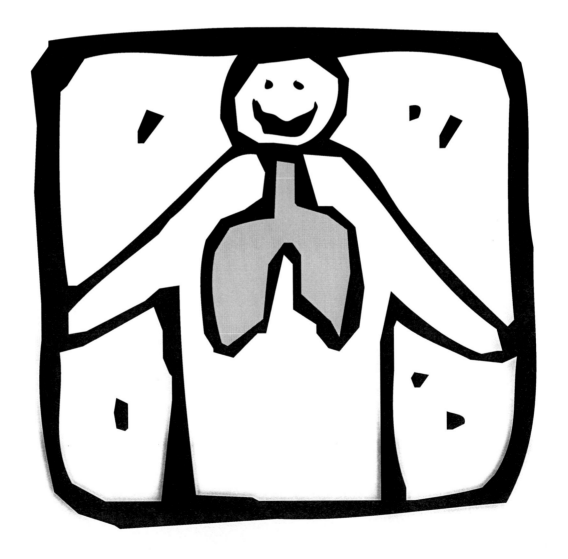

Learn to Relax

When you get nervous, your heart and lungs work

harder and faster. Try taking several slow deep breaths

while counting to yourself (inhale, 1 - 2 - 3 - 4 - 5,

exhale , 1 - 2 - 3 - 4 - 5). When your body slows

down, you'll be able to think clearly

and do your best work.

Think Positive Thoughts

I am prepared.

I can do this.

Think Positive Thoughts

Remember the classic children's story, *The Little*

Engine That Could? By repeating the positive

thought, "I think I can, I think I can.." the little train

was able to climb a big mountain. Think of a

positive statement you can think and say

to yourself at test time.

Prepare Your Body With...

Nutritious Food

Regular Exercise

Adequate Rest

Prepare Your Body

Taking care of your body is important every

day, not just on test days. But, your brain will work

better if you are well fed, rested and physically fit.

This may be a good time to discuss healthy and unhealthy eating habits, appropriate amount of sleep for children this age, and types of physical activity children are involved in.

Read Carefully!

Answer Easy Ones First!

Check Over Your Work!

During the Test

Read directions and questions carefully. Don't rush.

Answer the ones you know first.

This makes you feel good/builds confidence.

Always proof-read your answers. Check for errors,

omissions, double bubbles or stray marks.

Test Yourself on Test Anxiety

Do you get nervous and fearful just before a test? ❏ yes ❏ no

Which of the following are true for you? I get nervous about tests because:

- ❏ I don't know enough.
- ❏ I just panic even though I usually make good grades in school.
- ❏ I haven't studied or prepared.
- ❏ I always worry about things.
- ❏ I'm afraid of disappointing others.
- ❏ I'm afraid of embarrassing myself.

How anxious are you?

Put a number in each blank—1 for never, 2 for sometimes, or 3 for often.

_____ Right before a test, I have sweaty palms, shaky hands, or other visible signs of nervousness.

_____ I get butterflies in my stomach before a test.

_____ I feel queasy or sick to my stomach before a test.

_____ I look at the test and feel that I don't know any of the answers.

_____ During a test, my mind goes blank and I forget things.

_____ I have trouble sleeping well the night before a test.

_____ I make careless mistakes like skipping questions or putting answers in the wrong places.

_____ I have difficulty choosing answers.

_____ I remember the answers after the test is over.

_____ I panic at the thought of taking a test.

Add up your score. Scores will range from 10 to 30. A low score (10-15 points) means that you do not suffer from test anxiety. In fact, if your score was close to 10, a little more anxiety may be helpful to keep you focused and get your blood flowing during a test. Scores between 16 and 21 indicate a normal level of test anxiety. Scores above 22 suggest that you have a high level of test anxiety. You may need some help with test taking.

* Adapted from questionnaire by Nist and Diehl (1990), and The Center for Advancement of Learning, Muskingum College, 1998.

Coach Frank's Training Tips

1. **Develop a Relaxing Routine**

2. **Talk and Think Positively**

3. **Don't Get Stuck**

4. **Practice to Make Progress**

5. **Prepare Your Body Physically**

How Parents Can Help Children Do Their Best on Tests

The best thing you as a parent can do to help your child do his/her best on standardized tests is to provide positive support by expressing confidence in your child's ability to do their best. Let that be your expectation, as well. Children should know that test scores are important, but are not the measure of your love and acceptance of them.

On test days, try to provide a calm, stress-free environment each morning as your child gets ready for school. Get up in plenty of time to avoid morning rush and anxiety. Curtail nighttime extra-curricular activities and outings that may interfere with their regular bedtime routine.

Help teach and reinforce the following test-taking tips and strategies:

- **Get Plenty of Rest Each Night**
- **Eat a Good Breakfast**
- **Have a Positive Attitude**
- **Relax... Don't Fret**
- **Try Hard... Do Your Best**
- **Listen Carefully and Follow Directions**
- **Think Before You Answer**
- **Read Directions and Questions Carefully**
- **Don't Rush... Work at Middle Speed**
- **Check Over Your Work When Finished**
- **Don't Expect to Know Every Answer**

Resources and References

Nist and Diehl (1990). Test anxiety questionnaire. Adapted by The Center for Advancement of Learning, Muskingum College. New Concord, OH: 1998.

Piper, Watty. (1961). *The Little Engine That Could*. New York, NY: Platt & Munk.